The End Of Twilight
Mariah Archibeque
Illustrations by: Steven Archibeque

The End Of The Rose

By

Mariah Archibeque

CITIOFBOOKS, INC.
3736 Eubank NE Suite A1
Albuquerque, NM 87111-3579
www.citiofbooks.com

Hotline: 1 (877) 389-2759
Fax: 1 (505) 930-7244

Ordering Information:
Quantity sales. Special discounts are available on quantity purchases by corporations, associations, and others. For details, contact the publisher at the address above.

Printed in the United States of America.

ISBN-13:   Paperback   979-8-89391-455-9

Library of Congress Control Number: 2024924575

Table of Content

"It's okay to be different, because our differences are what makes us who we are."

- *Mariah Archibeque*

DEDICATION

"This book, The End Of The Rose, is dedicated to Mariah for all she went through having Ewing Sarcoma cancer; how Mariah fought and never gave up. Mariah wrote The End Of The Rose to inspire those to feel that they are not alone."

ACKNOWLEDGEMENTS

I would like to thank my family, editor and most of all my grandmother. I thank my mother a lot because she is one of the people who never gave up on me and wanted me to fulfill my dreams and not to give up on the things I love doing. I thank my grandmother a lot because she is the one who gave me the idea of writing a story. My mother and her encouraged me a lot to keep going and that I should never give up. There was a point in time where I wanted to give up on writing or enjoying the things I love. I was able to not give up because I had the inspiration and support of my family.

PROLOGUE

A peculiar young girl decided to venture into a forest on a soulless night when all things were broken and not found. Near a river she discovers a magical aura surrounding amysterious abandoned cottage. She leaves the forest and returns home, but she plans to go back to the forest another time. She returns to her Royal Kingdom and is ostracized because she is different from the other children...but even the purest hearts can be darkened and even the light within them can turn into something evil, maybe even a creature so powerful you'll never sleep again. This is where the story begins...

CHAPTER 1
Kingdom Come

In the Royal Kingdom there lived a girl named Karo Enika Medianoche, but for short, most people called her Karo. She was often playing in the forest when the gorgeous sunlight hit her beautiful glowing skin, running and exploring as if her brown eyes were caught in a haze, just as a child normally would. She has lovely black hair that flows behind her delicately like waves. She found a rather intriguing iridescent rose and took it home with her because she was rather fond of it. One of the generals of the knight's round table struck her because she was accused of practicing witchcraft. Instead of being hit on the hand she was struck in the face with the sharp spikes on the knight's armor that pierced like razor blades. The pain eventually subsided, however she was left with a scar on forehead that reminded her of that shameful day.

Karo, at about nine years old, ran off into the forest and discovered a house. A very strange house that was dark and gloomy which stood near the riverbank. She would often visit that area, because it reminded her of her mother's numerous stories about the land that once settled in silence there. As Karo walked onto the black, dark, and creaky porch, she found a small collection of magical items. She passes the magical items by, and curiously opens the front door. Karo stood in terror and stared at the woman who suddenly appeared before her. The small woman was wearing a white dress with navy blue flats, and her gray and white wavy hair was hanging loose at her shoulders. "Who are you?" the woman asked. Karo hesitantly began saying "My name is…" as the woman interrupted her.

"Nevermind I know exactly who you are!" the woman exclaimed.

"You do?" Karo asked confusingly.

"Of course I do," the woman said, as she looked down at her cauldron. "No need for an introduction, my dear, but I am Gladimere. Many have tried finding this place because they believe I could assist them in solving their problems, but they all failed. But that's not important right now," she says.

"Okay then, who am I?" Karo asks.

"The real question you should be asking is who you will become?" Gladimere says, pointing her skinny finger at her.

"I don't understand," Karo says.

"Child, I see dark forces in your path, but your fate will not change. For, those whom you thought were your friends will later on betray you," Gladimere foretold her as she disappeared.

As Karo left the house, she was confused by what she had just witnessed. She never had seen anything like that before. Gladimere was there, and then she was gone; just like that! As years passed by, Karo's nineteenth birthday was upon her, and she was betrothed to a prince named Alastair Valentine. Alastair, who was 19 as well, was from the northern kingdom where Karo was from. Alastair's blonde hair, broad shoulders, and charming smile entranced the damsels of the kingdom. They were also jealous of Karo who was soon to be his bride. She didn't let that stop her from marrying the prince. On the night of the party just before the wedding, a particularly incensed girl named Bethany, approached Karo and purposely spilled her goblet filled with dark red wine all over Karo's dress.

"What was that for?" Karo exclaimed, as she was furious at the girl for ruining her dress. "That was for stealing my prince," Bethany retorted.

"He wasn't yours to begin with and besides he chose me because he loves me for me and, unlike you, I'm not marrying him for the money, I'm doing it because…" Bethany cut her short, "because you have no choice and you don't love him, you only care about yourself, you may have had your coronation today, but don't act like that will last long!" Bethany smirks and brushes past her, shoving Karo out of her way.

Karo took a deep breath and headed to her room to get away from the party for a bit. Karo sat on her bed thinking, as she heard a soft knock on the door. "Come in," Karo said, as she opened the door. To much surprise and confusion, Karo is immediately surrounded by Bethany and her friends. "Hey, I wasn't aware that you were coming, Alastair must have summoned you to check up on me, he's always making sure that I am ok…" Karo paused for a minute as the damsels then began to corner her. "What are you all doing? Why are you trying to corner me and why do you have your hands behind your back? Bethany?" she questioned in fear.

"I told you your reign will not last long." Bethany said. "Alastair never asked us to check on you, instead we came to end things between you and him," she said as she was pulling out a knife.

"No I'm not going to let you, I will tell Alastair and the whole kingdom what you're trying to do," Karo asserted, trying to escape.

"I'm afraid that's not an option," Bethany says, pushing Karo down on the hard floor of the bedroom. "Get her girls!" she ordered as her friends started cutting Karo with sharp knives. Bethany and her friends kill Karo and leave her lifeless body, with blood pouring from the wounds and blood dripping from her eyes. Bethany runs to Alastair, letting him know of the tragedy, deceiving him as she tells him how she went to check on her and found her bloody body. She describes to Alastair how Karo laid dead on the floor of her bedroom, her eyes filled with nothing but blood, her dress with blood stains that covered the dark red wine Bethany spilled, and her face with cuts and slashes all over her body. Alastair ran upstairs to his bride's room, he was devastated to have found Karo gone. His heart broke in two, knowing his one true love was murdered.

"Who could have done this to you?" Alastair asked, as tears began to shed from his face. The knights rushed into Karo's bedroom and found her lifeless body on the hard floor near her closet in Alastair's broken hearted arms. Karo's father rushed upstairs to see what all the commotion was. He was distraught to see his daughter's lifeless body in Alastair's arms. He left without his daughter, to go make plans for her burial. A day later, the knights and Karo's father buried her next to her mother by an oak tree. The oak tree was a special place for her, her mother and her family where they enjoyed picnics under the shade. They would even all tell each other stories beneath the moonlight and the oak tree. For Karo it was a tradition to have small get-togethers for her family by the oak tree. But sadly, those traditions faded away after Karo's mother was killed, or so many have thought. The traditions vanished even more after poor innocent Karo was killed in cold blood. It indeed made it harder for the kingdom to bring back those traditions without Karo and her mother to celebrate them gracefully knowing that both had perished.

Late in the evening, Glademire crept into the cemetery, and left with Karo's coffin in which she lay. Glademire took Karo to her house and healed Karo with the exception of her cuts on her face. The cuts turned into scars and the blood in her eyes remained as her eyes glowed. As Karo awoke with such confusion, she wondered what had happened to her. Gladimere observed her and put a crown with chains that lingered, on Karo's head. "You may be wondering how you got here, how you're alive and what happened, well let's forget about that for your story is not yet over," Gladimere expresses, handing Karo a mirror. She gazes into it as she lifts her once white, but now black veil from her face and drops it as she tries to scream. However, nothing comes out, as her voice box has been damaged and the mirror shatters all over the floor.

"I know those girls betrayed you and I can feel your pain, but listen. What if I told you that I can take all your pain away if you will allow me to fix what has been lost and broken?" Gladimere questions.

Karo looks at her with confusion as she is handed a blood red rose from Gladimere. "Put this rose in the cauldron and it will show you your future and your path," Gladimere says. Karo walks over to the cauldron and drops the rose into it. She views the cauldron, trying to see her future without success. Disappointed, she looks down.

"What bothers you, child?" Gladimere asks while walking over to the cauldron and observing "Well this is odd, I guess only the living can see their future with a blood rose."

Suddenly, a necklace with a moon on it appeared.

"Well go on, take it, the necklace chose you." Gladimere says. Karo takes the necklace from the cauldron and puts on a red jacket that Gladimere hands her. Karo puts her veil down over her face and cries, but no sound comes out of her voice. "There's one more thing I'm forgetting. That necklace has many abilities, one of them being that you'll be able to speak once more and take those who wronged you and destroy their hearts. Now go, and take this blood rose and remind all of them who you are….Lady Midnight," Gladimere says, disappearing yet again.

Lady Midnight vanishes in the night soon after, looking to get revenge on those who wronged her. Little did Gladimere know that eventually karma would come and take its course.

CHAPTER 2

Once Was Lost, Now Is Broken

Centuries later, in the year 2022, a museum tour guide was explaining the story of the betrothed queen.

"This is boring, I mean there is no such thing as witchcraft or witches in general," comments a schoolgirl wearing a black leather jacket, a blue turtle neck shirt, black glasses and her hair up in a bun.

"I know you may think it's not real, but some would disagree," the tour guide replies.

"Yeah, yeah, whatever," the girl remarks.

"Well, what do you think really happened? Hmm..." the tour guide pauses as she reads the girl's name tag. "'Hmm, Lilith?" the tour guide asks.

Lilith starts speaking but made the decision of not responding back for some particular reason.

"That's what I thought, if you can't keep your mouth shut during a tour then you shall not be here at all," the tour guide scolded.

"Okay I'm sorry, but if it is true then where is she?" Lilith asks.

"Of whom are you referring?" the tour guide questioned..

"Karo, of course, if she is real then where is she?" Lilith questions.

The tour guide looks at the time and then back at her. "Times up, looks like that's the end of the tour, and it's time to close up the museum" the tour guide says, ignoring the question.

"You never answered my ques….," Lilith says, being interrupted by the tour guide. "End of the tour, now leave, nerd," the tour guide retorts, shooing her away. Lilith leaves and heads home thinking about the story the tour guide was telling.

After everyone left the museum, the lights start flickering and music from one of the exhibits starts playing. A security guard rushes over to the exhibit and looks around to see where the music was coming from.

Meanwhile, one of the voices warns,"You shall be punished for your crimes!"

He stood there perplexed as if there were ripples in his mind. "Is this some kind of joke? Who's there? Whoever you are, this isn't funny." The security guard directs his flashlight towards an exhibit. A figure wearing a black dress and red jacket appeared in front of the music box, which mysteriously kept playing by itself. She wears a golden necklace with a moon hanging from it. On her head is a crown with chains looped around it and attached to a black veil. Wearing black gloves she emerges from the dark in front of him. The security guard runs and tries to get help but the figure was too fast for him. Screams echoed throughout the exhibit hall in the museum. The security guard was never seen again, at least his body wasn't…

The next day officers surround the museum. A detective named Kea Lansky, walks over to the crime scene. Everyone she knew called her Lansky, but her family would just call her Kea. "Alright what do we have here?" Detective Lansky asks as she studies two eyeballs laying on the ground.

"It looks like the body is gone. All we've found are the eyes that might have belonged to an employee," a gloved officer conjectures, as he places the eyeballs in an evidence bag. "Well, how do you know?" Lansky asked, as she contemplated the contents of the evidence bag. Another officer strides over.

"Detective Lansky, we not only found eyes, and a flashlight, but we found this." The officer shows detective Lansky a crime scene photo.

"That's odd, it looks like writing in blood. But whose blood is the question?" she ponders, curious about what had happened the night before.

"Excuse me?" the officer asked.

"Nothing, I didn't say anything," Lansky comments before walking away. She asks a different officer at the crime scene "Are there any witnesses?"

"No, no one seems to have any recollection of what happened last night, or what happened to the security guard," the officer responds.

"Well it looks like we've got a murder and the more evidence we encounter, the more convoluted the clues become," Lansky declares, shaking her head. Lansky scrutinizes the photo while reading it to herself. "Excuse me? Miss….?" Lansky inquired of the tour guide.

"It's Cassie, what do you want?" Cassie rudely answered.

"I was wondering, what is that?" Lansky asks, pointing to the exhibit with a white veiled woman in a dress holding what appears to be a blood rose in one hand along with a partially exposed note in the other.

"That's a rose obviously, I don't see why that's of any importance to you." Cassie says.

"No, on the note in her hand." Lansky clarifies.

Cassie looks closely at the figure's hands and sees a piece of parchment with writing on it. "I don't understand…." Cassie pauses for a minute as a flashback of memories comes to her of the night her parents were presumed dead and she stood by her house crying.

"Excuse me? Hello? Cassie?" Lansky addresses her as she waves her hand in front of Cassie who had a blank stare on her face.

"What? Sorry I um…sorry I just remembered something. That note, it's just some old parchment paper that historians found and…well now it's here," Cassie hesitantly explains.

"Oh, okay, well I was just curious. It's just that the writing in blood one of the officers found, might be connected to the note. Sorry for wasting your time." Lansky says as she leaves the museum.

Cassie gulps and walks the opposite direction from Detective Lansky and the officers.

CHAPTER 3
Lies Unfold

A few hours go by and Lansky enters her house and thinks about what Cassie said about the note. She looks at the copy of the photo she got from the officer and reads what the writing says to herself. For some mysterious reason she could not understand the dates on the bottom of writing in the picture.

"The line of thieves will end." Lansky says as she pulls out her laptop and looks up the year 1686, to see what happened that year. "Hmm, what if it's not talking about thieves but the people who betrayed her and took everything from that poor girl shown in that hall of royals exhibit at the museum?" Lansky asks herself.

Lilith walks in and sees her sister on her laptop and is curious as to what she is doing.

"Hey Kea, what are you doing?" Lilith asks.

"Nothing, just work stuff." Lansky closes her laptop and puts it away in her bag. "It didn't look like work stuff, more like research on that boring exhibit that mean tour guide was explaining yesterday," Lilith says.

"Well if you must know there's been a murder at the museum yesterday and since you were there I figured you could tell me what you learned from that "boring" story you heard," Lansky says.

"From what I learned that girl was killed before her wedding day and they buried her in that outfit she was wearing at the museum, and also something about a note she wrote before she died, that's all I heard. "Why?" Lilith asks.

"It's not important, but anyways did you find out what the note says, by chance?" Lansky asks.

"Nope, I didn't really pay attention to that." Lilith says.

"I'm heading to my room, later Kea '' Lilith walks away to her room.

"Well she was no help." Lansky says as she pulls out her laptop and looks up the line of Valentines, learning more and more about them.

The next day, Lansky talks to the commissioner about the murders. "Look, this makes no sense Detective Lansky, the whole line of thieves could mean anything," the Commissioner says.

"Okay I've noticed a pattern here, some of the Valentines were killed and each time they are presumed dead, and it's all leading back to Karo Medianoche also known as Lady Midnight from those stories we've been told as children." Lansky says holding up an old newspaper.

"That's enough, I hate to say this but you're off this case, Lansky. This is a bunch of mumbo jumbo, something a crazy person would say," the Commissioner says as he puts the newspaper in the paper shredder and points to the door. "If you try to impede this investigation or even go near this case you will be fired," the commissioner demanded. "Fine, I promise I won't," Lansky says, exiting the commissioners office and walks outside seeing a girl strolling in the shadows. The girl had recognizable black high tops with a hint of green decorated with stars on the back of the heel. Lansky follows the girl and stops her. "You, I know it was you." Lansky says. "Fine I was the one who lowered the security guard in that exhibit but it was only a joke, only to prove that Lady Midnight doesn't exist, but I didn't know he would be killed," the girl says.

"So you did kill the officer? You're coming with me," Lansky puts handcuffs on the girl and walks her to the police station. Lansky walks in and talks to the commissioner. "I know you said not to impede or continue this case but I think I found who did it," Lansky says.

"This girl is responsible for that murder?" the commissioner asks, pointing to the tv. "This just in, there's been a murder at Holloway Museum, there have been no suspects or anybody there. The only thing officers found were eyes and a flashlight. But rumor has it there is something wicked lurking there, and Detective Lansky and other officers will keep us updated on this investigation, back to you Bobert." the news reporter says on the TV.

"Yes I believe this girl is responsible for the murder of that security guard, she told me herself." Lansky says.

"Yes it was me but I didn't kill the security guard. I only pretended to be Lady Midnight just to scare him so I turned on the music box. I didn't think my joke would kill him." the girl says.

"Well you did your job Lansky, I'll put this girl in our custody for now." the commissioner says.

"Wait I didn't kill him, there's more, I heard voices and weird sounds," the girl says in fear as she is taken away and put in a jail cell.

"That girl is innocent until proven guilty." Lansky says.

"That was until she started spitting out a bunch of crazy lies." the commissioner says. "But she said she didn't commit the murder, commissioner, maybe I was wrong. You can't put her in jail because she might know more about what happened," Lansky says. "Look, maybe it was a mistake putting you on this case or in charge of it. You should be proud of yourself, you caught the murderer and now she has to be sentenced for her crimes. And I said I'd put her in our custody, I lied she's going to the big house," the commissioner says.

"Wait, give me at least an hour to talk to her, just to find out more about what happened, and then I promise I won't impede on this investigation or question anyone anymore about it," Lansky says.

The commissioner thinks for a minute about what Lansky said before he can respond. "Alright I'll tell you what, I'll give you an hour to talk to her and if you can find anything that may have a lead on this case then I'll put you back on the case, but you would only have a month to investigate it, no more and no less, got it?" the commissioner says.

"I understand," Lansky says, as she walks out of the commissioner's office. Lansky walks over to the jail cell with some criminals who are to be transported to the county jail and she speaks to the girl. "I'm pretty sure you already know me, but I'm going to take you to the interrogation room for questioning, and then after that you have to be put back in the holding cell to get transported to the county jail." Lansky says to the girl as she takes her out of the cell and puts handcuffs on her.

"Look I didn't do it, I promise it wasn't me, there was someone else there," the girl says as she and Lansky head to the interrogation room.

Lansky and the girl walked in the interrogation room and the girl sat across from her so she could question her. "So tell me everything that you saw at the museum that night of the murder." Lansky says.

"Well I remember wearing a costume and waiting for the museum to close, and after everyone left I hid in the hall of royals exhibit behind the statue of Karo Enika Medianoche, from that story I heard." The girl started telling what happened at the museum and the specifics that she remembers.

"So that's when you turned on the music box?" Lansky asked, remembering what the girl said earlier in the alley.

"Well after I hid by that statue I walked over to this music box and yes that's when I turned it on," the girl said.

"Interesting, you mentioned voices heard, and someone else was there, can you tell me a little more about this?" Lansky asked as she was writing down everything that the girl had said so far.

"Well when I stood by the music box and I saw the security guard, I tried to scare him but then I heard someone's footsteps coming and voices.

The voices saying, "you shall be punished for your crimes and the line of thieves will end." I got so scared I ran into the hall next to the exhibit by the hall of royals," the girl said.

"Hmm so you're telling me that you heard someone else there with these voices, and whoever was there must have killed the security guard and not you." Lansky said, opening a file with photos taken from the crime scene.

"Yes and after that I heard the security guard screaming and then silence, nothing could be heard. So I went over to see what had happened. The security guard was gone, the only thing I found were his eyes." the girl said as she put her head down. "It's all my fault if I hadn't played that joke on that security guard none of this would have happened," the girl said, crying.

"I know it's not the right time to ask but was there anyone there with you that you knew?" Lansky asked. The girl puts her head up and looks at Lansky. "No, no one I knew, but before I ran off I did catch a glimpse of her reflection on this exhibit with a blood rose on it." the girl said.

"So it was a woman and can you tell me what you saw?" Lansky asked.

"I didn't see her face because it was covered by a black veil she had on but I did see she was wearing a crown that had a chain on it," the girl said, drawing an image of what she saw on the paper Lansky handed her.

Lansky looks at the drawing and examines it for a minute. "Interesting, and did she write the message on the wall in blood?" Lansky asked.

"I'm not sure I left the museum before I could see anything else happen," the girl said. "Thanks, that's all I needed to know," Lansky said as she uncuffs the girl from the table and the lights start flickering.

"Um, what's going on?" the girl asked in terror.

"I don't know, I'm not doing this." Lansky said. The lights go out and it turns pitch black in the interrogation room. Lansky turns on her flashlight and looks at the girl. "Hey are you alright?" Lansky asks.

"Yeah I'm fine." the girl said.

"Stay close, I'll find the light switch and see if I can turn the light back on." Lansky says. The girl follows Lansky to the light switch and looks around to see if there's anyone else there besides them. Lansky uses her flashlight to find the light switch and turns the light back on. When Lansky turned the light back on, there laid a blood rose.

"This can't be true, I don't understand," the girl said.

"What can't be true?" Lansky asked, looking at the rose on the table.

"The story of Lady Midnight, that blood rose was left there for a reason," the girl says. "Look if you're right then maybe I could convince the commissioner to let you go so we can see if Lady Midnight really is out there," Lansky says.

"There's no way he'll believe us or rather me, considering the stunt I pulled," the girl said.

"He'll believe me because he's my friend," Lansky says.

"Okay if you say so," the girl says.

Lansky walks with the girl and puts her back in the jail cell. She heads to the commissioner's office, but all she found were the eyes of the commissioner left on his desk. Lansky screams in terror for an officer. The officer walks in and sees Lansky and a set of eyeballs on the desk..

"Detective Lansky, where's the commissioner and what is going on?" the officer asked. "I don't know, but I think the same thing happened with the commissioner like it did with the security guard from the museum." Lansky said.

"Well looks like you better call this one in," the officer said as she opened the door and called in backup. "All units, we got a serious case, it looks like we got another murder…the commissioner," the officer said as a group of officers walked in the commissioner's office and started investigating.

CHAPTER 4
Lonliness

Back in 1996, Lady Midnight stood by the lake looking at her reflection and remembering the pain and heartbreak she went through after she died and was resurrected. Gladimere appeared in front of her. "You know I remember seeing that sadness and believe me it's not going to make your revenge easier," Gladimere says. Lady Midnight looks at her and chokes Gladimere with one of her hands. "Okay I admit I overstepped," Gladimere says as Lady Midnight lets go of her neck. "Thanks, I guess, well there's something you should know, after you died, the prince Alastair married that girl Bethany, and now there's a whole family of Valentines," Gladimere says. A tear is shed from Lady Midnight's face before thunder surrounds the area she is at and a huge magic blast comes out of her hands. And her eyes glowing even bloodier than before. "I will end their bloodline and take back what once was mine," Lady Midnight says as she realizes what Gladimere meant by the necklace giving her back her voice. Gladimere disappears into the dark parts of the forest.

In the present day, Lansky was still trying to solve the case but instead of one she had two cases to solve: the murder of the security guard at the museum and the murder of the

Commissioner. While she tried to solve the case she also became the new Commissioner. "This Just in: recently there's been a new murder, the murder of commissioner Doxen at the police station. Many believe it was a criminal let loose or one of the officers did it. No one knows for sure, but maybe the new commissioner, Kea Lansky knows because many say she was the last one to talk to him. Could this be connected to the murder that happened at the museum? That is it for now, back to you Bobert." the news reporter says on tv.

"I cant believe the mayor made me commissioner and now this case is in my hands," Lansky says.

"Well I believe it, you've been here the longest and the only one the commissioner liked," an officer says. "Now where did that girl go?" the officer asked.

"Well after what happened to the commissioner, the court found her innocent so they let her go as I had hoped," Lansky says.

"What do you mean by 'had hoped?" the officer asks.

"Nevermind not important, now what is important is solving this case," Lansky says.

"Alright, my team is on it, commissioner," the officer says leaving Lansky's office. Lansky sat in her new office and was trying to figure out more about the murders. She then got up and looked at the photos she placed on the bulletin board. "Hmm a security guard and a commissioner of the police station, this is odd." Lansky says to herself. "A commissioner and security guard? Hmm," she repeated to herself.

A woman with blonde hair, a leather jacket, jeans and a buttoned up shirt walks in.

"Sounds like you got a case on your hands," the woman says.

"Yeah how did you-who are you?" Lansky asks.

"I'm agent Effiney Linadale and I work for the FBI." Effiney says holding up her badge.

"Why are you here?" Lansky asks.

"Enough questions there's a riot started and some people are saying you killed the commissioner the other day," Effiney says.

"But I didn't kill him, I walked in and found his eyes on what used to be his desk," Lansky says.

"I know and I believe you but what I don't believe is why you let a criminal free," Effiney says.

"She is not a criminal, she is innocent," Lansky says.

"Well that's not what officer Judy Lockes says," Effiney says.

Officer Judy walks in wearing her police uniform. "I told you this would happen and you did not believe me," Judy says.

"Well since we're on this subject I think these murders are due to Lady Midnight," Lansky says.

"Prove it," Effiney says.

"Okay so I've been doing some research about these murders and they each happen every year. It dates somewhere back to the 1700s after the night she was murdered, she's only killing the line of one family, and that family is the Valentines," Lansky says.

"You sound crazier than a monkey on ice skates," Judy says.

"Okay the message an officer found said the line of thieves will end but what if its not talking about thieves but a family bloodline," Lansky says.

"I don't get it," Effiney says, confused.

"Lady Midnight was killed the night before her wedding day so she couldn't have had kids with Alastair Valentine but none other than Bethany Grace," Lansky explains as she points at the photos on the bulletin board. "And not only that but she was killed by Bethany and her friends because of jealousy," she says. "Hmm that all makes sense," Effiney says looking at the photos on the bulletin board.

"Exactly, so maybe we should have teams split up so we can investigate the locations further," Lansky says.

"Good idea, you do that and I'll go find that girl you let free the other day." Effiney says leaving.

"You are seriously out of your mind," Judy says exiting the room.

Judy gathers her team and starts to investigate the town hall to see what she can find. Judy hears footsteps and uses her hand to point to the direction of the footsteps and the sounds heard. A strange voice starts following the footsteps as music from the old record player starts playing in the mayor's office. "Okay Judy, this is just someone playing a prank on you, there is nothing to worry about," Judy says to herself quietly and slowly walks around with her flashlight.

"You should run," a voice said in the shadows.

A scream can be heard from the room next to the hallway Judy is in. "Oh no, this can't be good." Judy said, running to the mayor's office. "Hello, is anyone here?" Judy says, pointing her flashlight around the room.

Gladimere appears in front of her, smacking the flashlight from her hand. "You must be Judy Lockes." Gladimere says.

"And who are you? Someone who hasn't showered in weeks? Cause girl you stanky!" Judy says.

"Excuse me? How dare you insult me? I am way more powerful than you," Gladimere's voice echoed. "Okay my bad but why are you trying to scare the day life out of me? I'm way too smart to die young, I got bills to pay," Judy says.

"Look I am Gladimere, and I know about the murders and believe me you should not get in her way," Gladimere says.

"Well whoever you are talking about she's killing innocent people so she needs to stop," Judy says.

"Fine but don't come crawling back to me when you find the thing you value most gone," Gladimere disappears.

"Wow, the only thing I value other than my kids is my dog Pedro and he's lazier than a raccoon digging in the trash can," Judy says. "Now where did that girl Gladimere go, you know for such a strange woman she sure does walk fast," Judy says as she looks around. She finds someone's eyes left on the mayor's desk and a broken flash light. "I am so out of here." she says, hearing whispers.

"Why have you come?" one of the whispers says.

"Don't stop me or you will die," another whisper says.

"I'm leaving and I'm not coming back." Judy says, running out and dropping her flashlight on the ground. Lady Midnight appears from the shadows with what appears to be a blood rose. She walks around and looks at the painting of her childhood bully Bethany sitting next to Alastair. She slashes the image with a knife and places the blood rose on the floor and disappears.

Meanwhile at the museum, detective Lansky and her team investigate the hall of royals exhibit. The lights flicker and a woman appears next to detective Lansky. "You need to stop, before you are too late," Gladimere says.

"I don't have time for this," Lansky says to the woman. Voices from the shadows are heard from the end of the hall.

"I tried to warn you." Gladimere says, disappearing yet again.

"Who are you and what do you want?" Lansky says, pointing her gun and flashlight towards the end of the hallway.

"I will not answer that question," a voice said echoing in the shadows.

"You will not stop me and you can't," another voice said.

"So leave before I hurt the undeserving of being hurt," a voice said, echoing and getting deeper and deeper.

"No, look whoever you are. I know what it's like to lose someone you care about, I get it, but please don't make a mistake that will ruin everything you once had," Lansky says. Lady Midnight listens for a minute before screaming and destroying half the statues in the hall of royals exhibit area. Lansky drops her flashlight and passes out on the ground from how powerful the scream was. One of the officers drags her body out of the museum and puts her in the police car, driving them away to safety.

CHAPTER 5
My Shattered Heart

Lady Midnight held on to her necklace and she started to see a vision of her mother singing to her when she was a kid and what she told her. "What are you singing, mother?" Karo asked.

"Just a song my mother used to sing to me when I was your age," Karo's mother Evangeline said.

"It's very lovely," Karo said sitting next to her mother. "Do you promise to never leave me?" Karo asked.

"I promise, Karo, there will be a time where it will seem like I'm not there but I'll always be with you," Evangeline says smiling at her.

The knights barged in and took Karos' mother away from her, shouting, "witch!!!"

Karo tried to stop them but she was too late to save her mother. "Nooo!!!" she screamed. The vision faded and the more Lady Midnight remembered the more she realized how much torture she went through and how she'll never learn to forgive those who wronged her.

At the hospital, Lansky woke up and the first person she saw was Judy.

"Glad you're awake, girl, have I got loads to tell you," Judy says.

"How did I get here?" Lansky asks.

"Let's just say you passed out at the museum," Judy says.

"I don't remember that but anyways I better get on this case right away," Lansky says. "Alright let's go then," Judy says. Lansky gets up and puts her jacket on and walks out with Judy. She gets in Judy's police car and looks out the window as Judy is driving the car.

"How long was I in the hospital for?" Lansky asks.

"You've been there for about two weeks, whatever happened in the museum must have affected you badly, not severely just badly," Judy says.

"How is that not severe?"Lansky says.

"Well it is but it isn't, nevermind that, we got a case to solve," Judy says, pulling up to the police station. Judy gets out of the car with Lansky and they both head inside the building. Lansky walks in her office and sees Effiney sitting at her desk.

"Detective Lansky, what are you doing here?" Effiney says.

"I work here and I'm the commissioner so do you mind getting out of my desk?" Lansky asks.

"Yeah no worries I'll move but there's something you should know, after I questioned that girl you let go I started to realize that maybe you were right about the case and also there's been another murder. In the forest, I investigated it a little with some of my agents and none of them made it back to the FBI building," Effiney says.

"That's strange, I wonder why that is," Lansky says.

"I'm not sure but if Lady Midnight is real, then we really upset her this time," Effiney says, getting up from Lansky's desk.

"What do you mean by that?" Lansky asks, confused.

"Look I don't want to scare you but there's a girl who works in the museum whose parents were killed because they thought of stopping this wicked being but I'm not sure that happened because I wasn't working as an FBI agent at the time, you should probably look into that, who knows it might be a lead for this case," Effiney says walking out of Lansky's office.

"Hmm, interesting," Lansky says to herself. Lansky then decides to head to the museum to look for Cassie. As she walks in, she notices that there's a bunch of caution tape in the hall of royals exhibit area. She stands there for a minute and remembers hearing the screaming in the shadows, the pain, the suffering she endured, and also catching a small glimpse of the statue of Lady Midnight revealing what she looks like now, the truth about what really happened ages ago.

A girl walks over to Lansky and notices that she is looking at the statue of Lady Midnight. "That statue is very strange, isn't it?" the girl says to Lansky who happens to have a blank stare on her face.

"Oh, what?, yeah it is, I think I may have encountered that girl, that the statue is of," Lansky says to the girl.

"You have?, do tell," the girl says.

Lansky turns and looks at the girl, recognizing her from the police station a few weeks before she became commissioner. "You are that girl I let free, aren't you?" Lansky asks. "Yes but I'm trying to turn my life around and I too have been doing my own investigating on this case," the girl said.

"Oh, and did you find anything?" Lansky asks.

"I did indeed, meet me at this address at sundown tomorrow and I'll discuss what I found," the girl says, writing down the address to meet her at and handing it to detective Lansky. The girl then walks out of the museum before Lansky could say anything more to her.

"Um okay, I guess," Lansky says with confusion. She looks at the address the girl wrote down on a paper she handed her and puts it in her pocket.

She sees Cassie and walks over to her. "Cassie, right?" Lansky asks.

"Yes that's me, and you're Detective Lansky, we talked a few weeks ago just before I heard about that incident that happened here," Cassie says.

"If you're referring to the statues being destroyed and me passing out then yes I do remember that talk we had," Lansky says.

"I wasn't talking about that incident, well yes a lot of the statues were destroyed but there was also a report of a missing diadem. An artifact that was stolen from here, more specifically in this area of the museum," Cassie says, pointing at the exhibit with the broken glass and a dagger stabbed in on the spot of where the missing artifact used to be.

"I wasn't aware of that, do you know what artifact went missing?" Lansky asks.

"Well the diadem, um artifact was an emerald crown of the moon goddess Estrella. Which was given to none other than….," Cassie pauses as she gulps. "It was given to none other than Karo Enika Medianoche, aka Lady Midnight just before she was killed," Cassie says, taking a glance at the broken statue of Lady Midnight with caution tape surrounding it.

"On her coronation day," Lansky says.

"On whose coronation day?" Cassie asks.

"Well on Lady Midnight's coronation day, she was given her mothers crown who was said to have been a witch, which was why she was killed, so to speak," Lansky says. "Well no one knows for sure why Karos' mother was killed, only that she was killed for a crime she did not commit," Cassie says.

"No, that's exactly what happened," Lansky says.

"How would you know? you weren't there," Cassie says, placing her hands on her hips, glaring at Lansky. "Just because I wasn't there doesn't mean I didn't do my research on her family history before I got assigned to this case," Lansky says.

"Good point, now what's the real reason you're talking to me, I know you're not talking to me because you wanted me to tell you more about Lady Midnight's mother or her family history rather," Cassie says. "You're right, I didn't, I wanted to know what happened to you years ago, now before you ask, yes I do know some things about it but only from what a friend has said," Lansky says.

"Well if you must know, I was about twelve years old and I had just come home from school. I looked for my parents everywhere but I couldnt find them, so I called the cops. The cops came and searched the house, when they finished searching the house for them….," Cassie pauses as tears fall from her face. "They couldn't find them but what they did find was their eyes and a note attached to what looked like a blood rose. That's when the cops told me that they were dead, I didn't believe it so I walked outside my house and I stood on my front porch devastated from what I had just been told. And that's when I knew that Lady Midnight was real, and that I would be next," Cassie says, wiping her tears from her face. "So when you asked me about that note, that Lady Midnight was holding before her statue got destroyed and appears to have been changed, I do know what it is and what it says. You wouldn't understand because you were never there when my parents were killed that night," she explains to Detective Lansky.

"Look I may have not been there but I do understand, my parents died in a house fire and I blame myself for it every day of my life but it's not like I can turn back the clock and change what had happened, because even if I wanted to it would be impossible for me to prevent their deaths," Lansky says.

"You're right, you can't. I'm sorry I didn't know that had happened to you, I should have known better than to say that," Cassie says.

"It's fine, you didn't know, but anyways thank you for telling me what happened, knowing this might help me with this case..," Lansky states, pausing for a minute.

"Before I go, I was hoping I could ask you something," she says.

"Yes, of course, anything," Cassie says.

"By chance, do you have the note that was found at your old house?" Lansky asks. "Yes, in fact I always keep it on me as a reminder of what had happened to me years ago," Cassie says, pulling the note out from her pocket and handing it to Lansky. Lansky takes the note Cassie handed her and looks at it for a second. "Bravery and courage is what led me to my death and remember me for I have not been forgotten," Lansky says reading the note. "That's odd, here is the note back," Lansky says, handing Cassie the note back.

"Keep it, that may help you with solving this case," Cassie says, handing the note back to Lansky. "Thanks, Cassie, I will never forget this," Lansky says leaving the museum.

CHAPTER 6
Remember Me For I Have Not Been Forgotten

    A few weeks before Lansky woke up from being passed out, Lady Midnight appeared in the museum. The cameras glitched as she walked past each one of them when she headed to the hall of royals exhibit area. She saw her crown in a glass case with a security system of lasers surrounding it. A security guard walked in the area she was at, holding a flashlight. She blended in with the shadows as the security guard walked by. She reappeared by the exhibit, after the security guard had left. She destroyed the glass case with her crown in it and set off the alarm system. A security guard heard the noise and rushed over to the hall of royals exhibit area. Lady Midnight took the crown and placed it on her head. A steel cage dropped down, surrounding her, as the security guard walked in. "Hey that's not yours, whoever you are, this is not funny," the security guard said. Lady Midnight stood there for a minute not listening to a word he said. "Not listening to me, huh," the security guard lifted up her black vale from her face revealing her small golden moon marking on her cheek. Lady Midnight grabbed the very beefy security guard by the neck and threw him across the floor, causing one of the statues to fall on top of him. She threw the cage surrounding her the other direction away from the security guard and walked past him, wearing the crown she once lost.

Meanwhile, Effiney stood in the forest with her small team, and searched the area. She had her team split up and look for clues. She then looked around, and the wind blew, as screams could be heard. She ran over to see where the screams were coming from but she found nothing, not a sound. She tried calling her team, but no answer and none of them showed up. Gladimere walked over to her and stood in front of her. "I warned you something bad would happen just like I warned that girl, Cassie's parents, just before they were killed," Gladimere said.

"Who are you and what are you talking about?" Effiney asks.

"Funny you should ask that, which reminds me of a girl I once knew," Gladimere says.

"You didn't answer my question," Effiney says, pointing her gun at her.

"Ugh, fine, I'll talk, I'm Gladimere and I'm talking about that tour guide Cassie, her parents were killed because they got in her way," Gladimere says.

"Whose way?" Effiney asks.

"The same person that lost her diadem in this very spot due to someone trying to find her, of course they failed," Gladimere says.

"What kind of diadem do you speak of?" Effiney asks, putting her gun away. "Her emerald crown, which was her mother's, just before she was killed for being accused of being a witch," Gladimere smirks.

"Oh, well how do you know this?" Effiney asks.

"Because I just do, now I must be on my way," Gladimere says leaving.

Present day, at the Lansky's house, there was a fire but Kea was unaware of it. Lansky drove up to her street and saw the firefighters there at her house putting the fire out. "Why would they be….?" Lansky thought to herself. As Lansky pulled up to her house, she got out of her car and was asking where her sister Lilith was.

A nurse walked over to Lansky, and looked at her. "Kea, we put your sister in the ambulance, we don't know if she'll make it, she seemed to be hurt pretty badly with the wounds we saw on her," the nurse said as she got in the ambulance.

"She better be okay, and I'm coming with you," Lansky says as she opens her car door. "Alright, sounds like a plan," the nurse says, closing the back of the ambulance doors. Lansky gets in her car and follows them to the hospital. She then gets out of her car, as she arrives at the hospital with the ambulance and the nurses inside the truck. She follows them inside and sits outside the waiting room waiting for them to tell her if her sister is okay or not.

A doctor walked over to the waiting room holding a clipboard."Kea Lansky?" The doctor called out her name in the waiting room.

"That's me, I'm Kea Lansky," Lansky raised her hand.

"Come with me," the doctor says to Lansky and they both walk outside to the hall. "There's something I need to tell you…," the doctor tried explaining what was going on before getting interrupted by Lansky. "Tell me she's okay, I don't want to lose her, she's my little sister," Lansky said, more worried than she could have ever been.

"That's what I wanted to tell you, I'm afraid Lilith, your sister, didn't make it. She was too wounded to be saved and she lost too much blood, especially from her eyes," the doctor said.

"No, she can't be, that is a lie. I can't believe this," Lansky screams.

"I'm sorry but it is true, and there was nothing we could have done, commissioner," the doctor explained.

"I don't understand, I want to find more things in this case ... I never thought she'd be next," Lansky says devastatingly, as she sits on a chair in the hall.

"Look there's something you should know, and it's that the surgeons found a rose in your sister's hand, I think that might have had something to do with her death, I have to go but hopefully you'll find some time to reconcile," the doctor says walking away.

After Lansky got the devastating news from the doctor, she investigated her burned down house to see if there were any clues she could find. Effiney stood by a room with caution tape at the entrance, holding a teddy bear with a note attached to it. Lansky walks over and looks at Effiney. "Wherever danger is, you seem to follow it," Lansky says. "Well that is my motto, wherever danger is, I follow, but anyways I take it you used to live here," Effiney says.

"How did you guess?" Lansky asks.

"I found your teddy bear and it has a note with your name on it," Effiney says. "One, that's not my teddy bear, it was my sisters and two, what does the note say?" Lansky asks.

"It says, this is what happens when you ignore me, detective Lansky, next time it will be that FBI agent Effiney and then you, mind telling me what the hell that is about," Effiney says handing Lansky the teddy bear.

"I know who did this, remember that girl you questioned, the one I let go just after the commissioner was killed?" Lansky asks facepalming.

"Yeah?, she did this, I knew she couldn't be trusted, let's go before she hurts anyone else," Effiney says walking out of the house with Lansky.

Lansky and Effiney walk in the alley after leaving the house.

"Well, well, well, I see you got my message," the girl said, wearing a pink dress, blue high heel boots, a black jacket, and her hair in a ponytail.

"It wasn't even sundown, you had no right, none at all," Lansky says.

"Yeah but your sister annoyed me, so I chased her to your house and set the house on fire. She called those pathetic firefighters, they did come to her rescue but eventually were too late to save her, and who's fault was that?" the girl asked.

"It was yours," Effiney says.

"Wrong it was the detective or should I say Commissioner Lansky's fault, her sister was killed," the girl said smirking.

"No it wasn't, who even are you?" Lansky asks.

"Funny you should ask, because I'm Joelle Grace, a descendant of Bethany Grace and I am the real Lady Midnight, you see I'm the one who killed all those people in fact I covered my tracks, I only did what I did because Karo Media-what's her face stole everything my ancestor Bethany had so I decided to get my revenge because that stupid girl deserves everything that she had coming to he-," Joelle said trying to explain what happened to Karo but before she could, she got stabbed and her neck got snapped by Gladimere who stood right behind her the whole time. Lansky and Effiney backed away from Gladimere while pulling out their guns and pointing them at her.

"What a liar, such a shame, she had such a good soul but it was darkened by jealousy," Gladimere says. Lansky and Effiney look at her shockingly. "What? Someone had to do something about this girl, she was spilling out lies and apparently blood too. She thinks she's Lady Midnight. I resurrected that girl so I should know what she looks like," Gladimere says.

"Did you just say you resurrected her?" Lansky asks.

"Um no I said I gracefully floated like a bee," Gladimere lied.

"No you said you resurrected Lady Midnight" Effiney says.

"Um no, I didn't, do yourself a favor and stay away from her," Gladimere says.

"Look, Gladimere, right? By chance is there a way to stop her?" Lansky asks.

"No, I don't know nada," Gladimere lies even more while crossing her arms.

"Oh really then why do you keep telling us to stay away from her then?" Lansky asks.

"Not telling a single soul," Gladimere says.

"Fine don't talk, but my sister was killed by that girl you brutalized, so please help us, I've lost too much already," Lansky says, putting her gun down for a minute.

"Child I wish I could help you but-," Gladimere says thinking for a minute.

"But you can't, I understand," Lansky says.

"No I just don't want to, is what I was going to say, anyways you have a case to solve which I highly recommend you don't continue, by the way," Gladimere says.

"Fine I won't, you may not be able to help me but maybe this will convince you to," Lansky says holding up a blood rose.

"Ha, you think a silly rose is going to convince me to do anything, you are most indeed mistaken," Gladimere says.

"Its not just an ordinary rose, it's a blood rose you gave to Lady Midnight," Lansky says.

"How do you know that?" Gladimere asks.

"Because of stories we've all been told," Lansky says.

"If you are the legend Gladimere herself, how are you still alive?" Effiney asks. "Figures, and although I do like to be called a legend, well a good skin care routine will keep you looking this good forever, that's how," Gladimere says the last part sarcastically. "That's impossible," Effiney says.

"I'm kidding but seriously that's a hidden secret all together, but I will say this and that, if that is a blood rose I can't touch it, I'm sworn not to and if I do,...I...can't tell you," Gladimere says as she disappears in the fog.

"Where did the fog come from?" Effiney asks.

"I dont know but we have to get out of here," Lansky says. "Agreed," Effiney says as she walks away from the fog with Lansky.

As they walk out of the fog, they end up in the forest. "Okay, how did we end up here?" Lansky asks. "Beats me, but this is the same area that my team disappeared at and I encountered Gladimere," Effiney says.

"Funny you never mentioned you encountered her," Lansky said.

"I didn't think it was important," Effiney says.

"True, but anyways, did you happen to have run into a house on your way in the forest?" Lansky asks. "No, why do you ask?" Effiney asks.

"That," Lansky points to the house in the dark part of the forest.

"Well that's a little unnerving," she says as she looks at the direction Lansky is pointing too.

"I couldn't agree more, maybe we should check it out, it may have more clues on this case," Lansky says walking further into the forest.

"Fine since you got me into this mess," Effiney says following her into the forest. As they walk further in the forest, Lansky calls her co-worker and trusted friend Judy at the police station.

CHAPTER 7
The Letter

Back at the police station, Officer Judy was talking to some of the officers and laughing with them. Until…suddenly she hears the telephone ring and she walks over to answer it.

"This is the Hollow Way police station, what's the emergency?" Judy asks.

"Judy, its me Lansky, I think I found a le-," Lansky says on the phone as the power goes out in the police station.

"Lansky, you there? Hello?" Judy asks confusingly.

"Looks like the power is out," an officer says, flashing his flashlight at her. "Obviously, and don't flash me with your light, that thing is very bright," Judy says, turning on her flashlight. "This is strange, the same thing happened in the museum from what Lansky said," Judy says, walking around trying to find the power switch. "Split up we may find a light or a way out," she says. The other officers split up and looks for a way out and a light switch. Judy walks around with her gun and flashlight. As she walks around, she hears footsteps, the same footsteps from the museum. A voice calls out to her, "Judy?" the voice says.

"Whoever you are, this isn't funny, yet again," Judy says. She follows the voices and the footsteps which lead her to the commissioner's office.

She opens the door and there she sees Joelle sitting in the commissioners desk. "Hello Judy," Joelle says. "How do you-, who are you?"Judy asks.

"Doesn't matter, but what does matter is I finally destroy Lady Midnight once and for all, I'll make sure she stays in the ground, you wait and see," Joelle gets up from the desk and walks over. "It's time this city knew what she had done, killing the lives of my family who did nothing to her," Joelle says.

"Actually she was killed by people who were cruel to her," Judy says, pointing her gun at her.

"Lies,lies and more lies, I don't believe you and I never will, in fact I will have my reveng-," Joelle says as she looks at Judy who seems to be paying attention to something else at the moment. "I'm trying to talk and it doesn't seem like you're paying attention, what is so important to you-," Joelle feels something tap her shoulder as she turns around and there stood Lady Midnight who did not look too happy to see her. "Oh sh-," she says but right before she could finish speaking her eyes got stabbed by Lady Midnight and her head got ripped off her body. Judy took her gun and shot at Lady Midnight but with every bullet she shot, Lady Midnight healed very quickly from the wounds.

"That's impossible, no one can heal from that," Judy says.

"It's not impossible," Lady Midnight says, her voice echoing. "You should have stayed away," she said with her voice echoing even more. She disappears in the shadows and things in the room start flying towards Judy. Guns from the glass case float towards Judy and point at her. "This can't be happening," Judy says.

Meanwhile back in the forest, Lansky and Effiney stood in front of the house they found. "Any word from your colleague?" Effiney asks, standing on one side of the door holding her gun, pointing it down.

Lansky stands on the other side of the door, holding her gun the same way. "No, the call must have been blocked due to how bad the service in this forest could be," Lansky says. "That's strange my phone signal works perfectly fine here, I don't see why yours wouldn't," Effiney says.

"Hmm, that is strange, when you say it like that," Lansky says, waiting to give the signal to go into the house. She gives the code, four signs with her hand. Her and Effiney break down the door with their shoulders hitting against it. Effiney picks up a rock and throws it towards the cauldron, she sees in front of her and Lansky, near the entrance of the house, to see if anything would happen.

"It's all clear," Effiney says as a door opens by itself.

"That's strange, let's go and investigate," Lansky says.

"Alright," Effiney says, following Lansky to the room with the opened door in the corner behind the cauldron. As they both walk in the room, the door shuts by itself making an old creaking noise as it does.

"That was even more strange," Lansky says, looking back at the closed door. "Yeah but I've seen this in a movie once, two cops enter a creepy house to investigate, a door shuts on its own and the two cops never make it back, the only difference between you and me in this scenario is that I'm an agent and you're a detective, well technically the commissioner but still," Effiney exaggerates a bit. "True but I think you're just being a little over exaggerated a bit, with the last part," Lansky says looking at the closet on one side of the room.

"Maybe, but I think it could still happen," Effiney says, putting her gun down on top of the dresser and opening one of the drawers. She looks inside to see what may be in it. "Maybe but I doubt it. Anyways, did you find anything over there?" Lansky asks, trying to open the closet but there's a lock on it.

"No, but I did find this blood rose with a letter attached to it, though," Effiney says, putting a glove on and taking the blood rose with a letter attached to it out of the drawer. Lansky walks over to dresser Effiney is at, curious about the letter. "What does the letter say?" Lansky asks.

"It says, Dear Karo, I am so happy we got to meet today. I know we haven't talked in a while since I moved but I figured writing on this piece of parchment might be a good way to talk. I almost forgot to tell you that I found something out about that rose you found in the forest. It's a rose that allows only the living to see their future or so I've been told. Well, hopefully I'll see you at the market today. Sincerely, your friend Lilith V.," Effiney says, as she finishes reading the letter and puts it down on top of the dresser.

"Lilith V.? Who do you think that could be?" Lansky asks.

"Hmm, I'm not sure but this note was written in 1696, so it must have been before the princess's coronation," Effiney says.

"This letter mentions Karo, the only person I could think of is Karo Enika Medianoche, aka Lady Midnight," Lansky says, walking over to the closet with a lock on it, holding the lock. Effiney shoots the lock on the closet door, almost hitting Lansky. "Are you kidding me? You could have shot my hand off," Lansky says, taking the now broken lock off the closet door.

"But I didn't, so you're fine, don't be such a baby," Effiney says, blowing the smoke from her gun away from it as she puts it away.

"I am no-, nevermind let's get back to investigating," Lansky says opening the closet and to her surprise she found a diary and clothes in it.

Effiney walks over to Lansky with a bag of powder she found in one of the drawers.

"Whoa, this is the dress Karo wore when she was meeting Lilith V. at the market," Effiney says looking at one of the dresses in the closet.

"Yeah and it looks like it has just been recently worn which means someone either lives here or has been hiding here," Lansky says looking at the dress.

As they both keep looking in the closet a door from the outside opens. "Someone is coming, hide," Effiney says hiding in the closet.

"Okay but where to whoa," Lansky says, being pulled in the closet by Effiney and she closes the closet door. A woman wearing a white dress with long sleeves walks in the room Lansky and Effiney are in. The woman looks in one of the drawers and notices the letter has been moved. She then looks at the closet door and sees the lock on the floor. "Someone has been here," the woman says walking out of the room as she shuts the door from behind.

"Isn't that the same woman who killed that girl in the alley?" Effiney asks.

"Yeah, before she disappeared in the fog which led us here, I noticed she had something shiny in her bag, like a trinket or something," Lansky whispers softly and quietly.

"Interesting that could explain why she was in the alley," Effiney whispers back.

The woman walks back in the room and picks up the lock from the closet. "I know you're here and I know why you came," the woman said.

Joelle appears by the woman and stands there placing her head back on her body. "Good now tell me, Gladimere, how did you resurrect Karo Enika Medianoche and turn her into Lady Midnight," Joelle says. "I'm not telling you and I never will, you wouldn't understand, that poor girl lost everything she had and I only did her a favor by bringing her back so she could get revenge on those who wronged her, and I thought you were dead," Gladimere says.

"You can't kill me and even if you tried it would be impossible to, now talk or I will use this blood rose to convince you," Joelle says holding up a blood rose.

"No, I don't know what you are or why you're trespassing in my home but you need to go, be gone or face my wrath," Gladimere says.

"Fine, but don't expect me to be so nice the next time I return," Joelle says walking out of the room.

"Yeah, whatever," Gladimere then continues to look around but as she does she senses another presence in the room. She walks to the closet and opens it. "What are you two insignificant idiots doing here?" Gladimere asks, looking at Lansky and Effiney. "Well we ended up in the forest from all that fog then we found what appears to be your house and-," Lansky explains, before being interrupted by Gladimere. "Hmm, okay that makes sense, I see you found the letter from a girl named Lilith Valentine," Gladimere says.

"Karo's best friend and also the sister of Alastair, what do you know about her and why did you lie to us earlier about you resurrecting Lady Midnight?" Effiney asks.

"I'm not going to say, I told you to stay away and to not interfere and what did you two arrogant fools do, you intervened and now you're too late," Gladimere says, her voice echoing.

"What's that supposed to mean?" Lansky asks.

"One of your allies will die and so will you," Gladimere says, trying to disappear but ends up back in the room.

"You can't leave this house, every time you disappear you end up back in this room, why?" Effiney asks. "Again I'm not saying," Gladimere says as blood starts dripping from the roof of the house.

"Fine, don't say anything but more people will die if you don't," Lansky says.

"I don't care and even if I did I wouldn't have a heart anyways," Gladimere says. "A heart? Someone stole it from you which is why you can't touch the blood rose," Effiney says.

"No stupid, that's not why I can't touch the blood rose you wouldn't understand and I shall not tell you," Gladimere says.

"First off I'm not stupid, second not all blondes are stupid as that is just a stereotype, and third what's with all the dresses, the diary in the closet and this powder?" Effiney asks. "It's none of your business now so leave," Gladimere says as fog appears. Lansky and Effiney try to see where Gladimere is but by the time the fog cleared they ended up back in the police station. Lansky walked around and noticed that the power was out. "I knew something odd was going on here, that explains why the phone cut off earlier," Lansky

says.

"Yeah," Effiney says as she hears gunshots coming from Lansky's office. "Somethings going on, let's go," she says as she follows Lansky to her office.

As they walk in, Effiney and Lansky see Judy trying to block the floating guns shooting at her with a trash can lid. Judy sees Lansky and Effiney walk in. "Thank goodness you two arrived, now may not be time for a friendly reunion right now because I'm dealing with something right now," Judy says.

"Okay we're here to help," Effiney says, shooting at the weapons floating in the air attacking them.

Lansky stands next to Judy who happens to be holding a trash can lid. "Might not be a good time to ask but where did you find the time to get a trash can lid?" Lansky asks.

"You never know what you might find in the dark," Judy says.

The weapons drop on the floor and Lady Midnight appears in front of them. "Oh no this can't be good," Judy says.

"The stories, all the legends were true," Effiney says.

Judy runs over to Lady Midnight and attacks her. Lady Midnight grabs her by the neck and throws her across the room as Judy runs towards her. She then lifts her veil up from her face, revealing a face that was once forgotten but now remembered.

"Please don't do this," Lansky says.

"I have my rights and you can't stop me," Lady Midnight says as her voice echoes. She screams, causing the building to collapse. She then scratches Effiney with her hand when she floats down and floats past her very quickly.

"Let's go before the building falls on us," Lansky says as she starts to drag Judy out the door.

"Okay," Effiney says following Lansky out of the building. As Lansky and Effiney make it out of the building, the police station collapses.

"I was not expecting that," Lansky says.

"Me neither," Effiney says looking at her wound on the side of her chest. She falls down but before she hits the ground Lansky catches her.

"I'm not going to let you die on me, I'll call for help," Lansky says, sitting on the floor gently placing Effiney's head on her arm.

"No, I think you've done enough to help me," Effiney says, coughing while she is slowly dying.

"No, please I've lost too much, I don't want to lose my friend too," Lansky says, reaching for her phone to call for help.

Effiney stops her with her hand. "It was a pleasure working with you, Kea," Effiney said before she died. "Effiney? Effiney? no, no, please, don't go," Lansky says with tears falling down her face. "NOOOOOO!" Lansky yells while crying.

Judy wakes up from being passed out and walks over to Lansky. "I can't believe this, she was such a good soul," Judy says sitting next to Lansky hugging her.

CHAPTER 8
If Only I Had Known

A few days later at the funeral of Effiney Linadale, Lansky stood near a tree watching the people by Effiney's grave. "It's not your fault, Kea," Judy says, walking over to Lansky. "It is and I should have stopped Lady Midnight when I had the chance, and now her family is standing there looking down at me for what I have done," Lansky says. "There's something you should know, and that is that those people are not her family," Judy says.

"What do you mean?" Lansky asks.

"I read Effiney's file the day she first came to the police station and I found out something about her," Judy says.

"What did you find out?" Lansky asks.

"Well it said that her birth parents were killed in a car crash that happened years ago, I had to look into that more because I remembered hearing about that from another officer," Judy pauses, and then continues. "So I went to the orphanage the officers told me Effiney was at, when she was a kid. The owner of the orphanage had told me Effiney said they were on their way back home. And their car got wrecked and it flipped over. She survived but unfortunately her parents didn't. She ended up in the system because she had no one left," Judy says.

"But she did get adopted though, right?" Lansky asks.

"From what I heard she did, but her adopted parents did all they could but as she got older, they neglected her and she ran away from home. My guess is that those people over there are her adopted family members or some of her friends," Judy explains.

"Why would they be here?" Lansky asked.

"Some of her adopted family members cared for her but Effiney didn't really say anything about this, I found out from investigating it myself," Judy says.

"If only I had known, I wouldn't have been so worried about whether or not she was dangerous," Lansky says with guilt.

"Don't put yourself down like that, you didn't know, anyways what do we do now, boss?" Judy asks.

"I'm not your boss, I may be commissioner but I don't feel like I've earned that right yet," Lansky says.

"It's fine, I understand but what's the plan?" Judy asks.

"Well we got three people to take down now, Joelle who killed my sister, Lady Midnight who killed our friend Effiney and Gladimere whose suspiciously hiding something, were going to need more help on this, we need to find out what Gladimere's motives are," Lansky adds.

"Good point, we could try the elderly home, I did hear one of the ladies there talk about something that may have some relations to the case," Judy says.

"Alright we'll go there now," Lansky says. Lansky and Judy get in the police car and head to the Holloway Home for the Elderly.

Judy turns on the radio and starts jamming out to some music. Lansky turns the radio off and looks at Judy for a second.

"Hey, I was listening to that," Judy says.

"Listening to music while there's a case to solve is not really necessary," Lansky says.

"Who's driving you or me? Huh, I'm trying to get comfy," Judy says.

"You are, what's your point?" Lansky asks.

"Well the driver picks the music, so I'm going to listen to music to get my mind off the case for a bit, just until we get to our location," Judy says, turning on the radio and a song comes on, a song that Lansky heard when she was a kid.

"I remember this song, it was my parent's favorite," Lansky says.

"Yeah, I remember your mom and dad told us that it was a song they listened to back when they were in highschool," Judy says.

"Yeah, it was their song," Lansky said, looking out the window.

"Yeah, what happened to you? You used to jam out to music all the time, that was until you became well like you carry so much guilt," Judy says as she continues to drive. "I guess after my parents death, it changed me, like I became a person who has so much guilt I can't let go of it, especially after my sister was killed," Lansky says, putting her head down.

"Look none of it was your fault, you can't put yourself down like that because in the end you'll just keep fading like a rainbow after it rains," Judy said.

"You got that from my mom, and you're right," Lansky says, putting her head up.

"Yeah, you know I'm right, but anyways we're here," Judy pulls up to the elderly home and parks the car.

A body falls down on the car cracking the front windows of the police car. Judy and Lansky get out of the car and run inside. "Well that was unexpected," Lansky says.

"Yeah, agreed," Judy says.

A woman walks over to them wearing a pink polo shirt, a butterfly barrette in her hair, a smile on her face and jeans. "Hi, can I help you, Officer Judy, Commissioner Lansky?" the woman asked, while holding a clipboard in her hand.

"Yeah, we're looking for a lady by the name of Gunderson?" Judy says, looking at the woman.

"Oh, she's over there playing checkers by herself, any particular reason why you need to see her?" the woman asks.

"We're trying to solve a case," Lansky says.

"Oh, well I'm Chanel and if you need anything else let me know," Chanel says, walking away.

Lansky and Judy walk over to the lady playing checkers by herself. "Hey, Miss Gunderson, I was wondering if we could ask you some questions," Judy says. "Yes, of course you can. Please, call me Lacey," Lacey says, placing a black checker piece down on the board.

"We were wondering if you knew anything about the legend of Gladimere?" Lansky asks.

"How do you know that name?" Lacey asks in a scared tone.

"We may have encountered her, why is everything alright, ma'am?" Judy asks.

Lacey looks around before speaking. "Follow me, there's something I need to show you," Lacey says getting up.

"Um okay," Lansky says, walking with Judy, following Lacey to a room. Lacey walks in the room with both Lansky and Judy. "Is this your room?" Judy asks while looking around.

"Yes, but this is what I wanted to show you," Lacey says, holding up a book.

"A bedtime story?" Judy asks, very confused.

"No, it's a book on Gladimere but mainly Karo Enika Medianoche. You see, Karo's mother was killed for people claiming she was a witch but that was only because Gladimere told everyone she was," Lacey says, opening the book, showing Lansky and Judy the pages.

"And was she a witch?" Lansky asks.

"Yes she was, but no one knew, only her dear friend Gladimere knew. But after she was killed, Gladimere was said to be cursed and if anything bad were to happen to Evangeline's daughter, she was forced to remain in her house never to use her magic outside of it," Lacey says.

"Well something did happen to her and now she has been resurrected and we don't know how to stop her," Lansky said.

"Look, I wish I knew but I don't know, no one does. But I do know this, you can't thaw a heart that's been broken and darkened, it remains the same," Lacey says, closing the book and putting it away. "Gladimere's motives were always the same, power, and reven-,"

Lacey says as her throat is slit and she falls to the ground.

Joelle appears behind Lacey. "I always knew I couldn't trust her to keep her mouth shut," Joelle says.

"Shouldn't you be dead?" Judy asked.

"I can't die, no one can kill me," Joelle says, walking to the closet and opening it.

"You're not a Grace are you?" Lansky asks.

"How did you figure it out?" Joelle asks, looking for something in the closet. "Well I saw you at Gladimere's house and it seemed like you had elf ears, no one of the Grace family members has elf ears, so what are you?" Lansky asks.

Joelle closes the closet and puts a mask on. "Lets just say I'm someone you don't want to mess with," Joelle says as the eyes on her mask glow and she throws Lacey's body out of the window.

"No, we could have saved her, what's the real reason you're doing this?" Lansky asks. "Lady Midnight gets all the fame, the glory, so I messed with her life line causing her to have the fate she solely deserved. Gladimere became more fond of her than me. So I offered her childhood bully a deal she couldn't refuse, she then took my offer and well she became Queen of the Hollow Way Kingdom. And all the glory was hers, that was until Gladimere decided to resurrect Lady Midnight," Joelle says.

"So you then posed as a descendant of Bethany Grace, that way you can have all the attention on you," Lansky says.

"Correct now I better go, time sure does pass when you're having fun," Joelle says, disappearing.

"Well now we know what Gladimere's motives are and that we may have some way of stopping her, Joelle and Lady Midnight," Lansky says.

"Yeah but we don't have anyone left who can help us, the one person we had is now dead.

And suspiciously not on the ground anymore," Judy says looking out the window. "That's strange, but anyways we better go, I might know someone who can help us," Lansky says.

"Okay I'm coming," Judy says following Lansky out of the room. Lansky and Judy walk outside and notice their car has been wrecked. "Well it looks like we're walking," Judy says.

"Oh, boy," Lansky says.

A few hours later, Judy and Lansky make it to Cassie's house. Lansky rings the doorbell to see if anyone is home. Cassie hears the doorbell and opens the door. "Detective Lansky, Officer Judy, I wasn't expecting you, what brings you by?" Cassie asks.

"I was hoping you could help us with a case," Lansky says.

"Oh, well come in," Cassie says. Lansky and Judy walk in the house. "So what can I help you with?" Cassie asks.

"Well, okay I'm just going to say it, we need your help with stopping Lady Midnight," Lansky says, taking a deep breath.

"I had a funny feeling that's what you came here for," Cassie says.

"You knew we were coming? How?" Judy asks.

"It's just, I may have encountered her when I was a kid, before my parents were killed, I just never knew why, but now I do. I am a descendant of Alastair Valentine and Bethany Grace and I now know why Lady Midnight is after me and the rest of my family," Cassie says looking at her tapestry of her family tree. "If my ancestor Bethany didn't murder that poor innocent girl Karo, none of this would have happened," she says, placing her hand on the tapestry, looking down.

Lansky walks over to her and places her hand on her shoulder. "I know how hard it is to live with so much guilt because of what your ancestors did but that's in the past, we can't stay in it forever because as my mom use to say you'll fade like a rainbow if you put yourself down for trying to live with so much guilt," Lansky says taking her hand off Cassie's shoulder.

"Thanks, I guess you're right," Cassie says, wiping a tear off her face.

"Are you related to Bethany Grace and Alastair Valentine?" Judy asks, looking at the tapestry hung on the wall in the living room.

"Yeah, and sometimes I wish I wasn't, mainly because a lot of my family members are dead, bodies missing, only things that anyone could find was eyes and a blood rose. The rarest flower in the world, it's said to be the most powerful rose in the world. Historians have been trying to get their hands on one but failed because they couldn't find one. So seeing one for myself as a kid was kind of crazy and I didn't fully understand until now," Cassie says sitting down on the couch.

"Well the blood roses have been seen very often now, with each murder and the disappearances," Lansky says.

"I know I've seen them on the news," Cassie says, holding up her phone, showing a video of a blood rose seen.

"Looks like it's all over social media too," Judy says, scrolling through her phone.

"That's interesting and a bit strange," Lansky says.

"Well anyways, let me know if there's anything I could do to help," Cassie says, putting her phone away. "We need help to stop Lady Midnight, Joelle, and Gladimere," Lansky says.

"Okay, Joelle is easy to send her back to where she came from, Gladimere finds the one thing she fears the most and uses it to stop her, and as for Lady Midnight no one knows," Cassie says.

"Okay well I hate to say this but we're going to need to split up," Lansky says. "Hold up, why would we need to split up? We don't even know Lady Midnight's weakness, y'all are nuts," Judy says.

"Good point, which is why I'm going alone to find out what that may be, while you two find the one thing Gladimere fears the most and a way to send Joelle back to where she came from," Lansky says.

"Alright, but just in case none of us survive I would just like to say that it was an honor working with you," Judy says.

"Same with you Judy, but now is not a good time for last words," Lansky says.

"Good point, now let's go and gear up." Judy says.

CHAPTER 9
The Unforgiven

After Lansky, Judy and Cassie gear up, they then split up to different locations. Judy went into the forest to look for the house Lansky sent her the coordinates to. Cassie was sent to the library to see if she could find anything on Joelle. While Lansky went to an asylum to see if anyone there knows anything about Lady Midnight.

Cassie explored the library to find anything she could on Joelle. The mystery and the thought of finding out about her was a bit unnerving for her. As she searched she found nothing but books on the legends and lore of Christmas. "There's nothing in this library that mentions Joelle," Cassie says as she searches the books. She walked past some books on the aisle she was at until she came across one, a book that said the unforgiven soul. She takes the book off the shelf and looks through it. "This may not have anything on

Joelle but this does have the info we need to defeat Lady Midnight and Gladimere," Cassie says, taking a picture of the page with a blood rose and a woman holding it. She then puts her phone away and sees a book fall from one of the shelves. She walks over and picks up the book off the floor. She opens it and looks through the book. "The history and lore of dark elves born on Christmas day," Cassie says reading the title of the book. "But what does this have to do with Lady Midnight and Gladimere?" she asks herself confusingly. As she looks at one of the pages in the book, the pages start flipping by itself until it hits the page with Joelle on it. "Whoa, she is the daughter of Krampus who sealed the fate of Karo and made sure she was to die in order for her to be resurrected as Lady Midnight so Bethany Grace could have the throne. The only thing to stop her is by giving her back the one thing that was taken from her," she reads to herself quietly as she puts the book in her bag without anyone looking and running out of the library.

Meanwhile, Lansky walked into the insane asylum to see if anyone there knew anything about Lady Midnight, and to her surprise someone did but not someone she was expecting to be there. Her Aunt Vivian, who was sent there by mistake for muttering what seemed to be some crazy stuff she has "seen." Lansky walked over to her Aunt Vivian who happened to be sitting by the window, glancing at the view outside. "Aunt Viv-," Lansky said, being interrupted.

"Kea, what a surprise, I haven't seen you since your parents' funeral. Judging by why you're here, I'm guessing you didn't come here for a little reunion," Vivian says. "No, unfortunately I didn't. I came because I heard you were sent here because you were accused of seeing a supernatural being who goes by the name Lady Mid-," Lansky says, being interrupted by her Aunt Vivian.

"Look I don't know if that's what I saw but what I do know is she did indeed seem like her though," Vivian says.

"What do you mean by seem?" Lansky asks.

"Well, I never told anyone this but before I ended up here, I saw things that no one else did, things that would only seem like fairy tales in a book or things that no one else can see," Vivian says.

"That explains why the rest of our family thinks you're crazy," Lansky said. "True the rest of our family always thought I was crazy but that never stopped me from doing the things I wanted to do before I lost everything and ended up here," Vivian says, placing her hand on her necklace.

"That necklace you wear around your neck, is that the reason you can see these things?" Lansky asks. "Well legend has it anyone wearing it will have good luck, and to answer your question no, and as for Lady Midnight I have heard stories but each one was different." Vivian says take her necklace off.

"How so?" Lansky asks, and takes out her notepad to write information down. "One story I heard really made me think, and it's the fact, a myth like Krampus, would have a daughter who would be so cruel to punish an innocent soul like Karo and made sure that she would become this being so powerful no one could stop her and there has been others but none like that," Vivian explains handing Lansky her necklace. "Take this, it may protect you and anyone around you from evil," Vivian says.

"You want me to have this? But you need this more than I do. I mean look where you are, this place is way more dangerous than any case I've dealt with," Lansky says, handing it back to her.

"No, I want you to have it. I've been here for eighteen years, long enough to be able to handle myself in this place and not need any luck or any protection by this trinket."

Vivian says, putting the necklace around Lansky's neck.

"This looks similar to the necklace Lady Midnight wore before she was murdered, it can't be it, can it?" Lansky asks, looking at the necklace.

"It could be, this necklace has been passed down in our family from generation to generation, none can really tell. But enough of that, you have to go now, my time out here is up," Vivian says hugging Lansky, saying her goodbyes before walking away. Vivian stops and then walks back to Lansky. "There's something I forgot to give you, it's a letter I wrote to your sister Lilith." she says handing Lansky the letter in an envelope. Lansky looks down as she takes the envelope from her Aunt Vivian. "What is it Kea?" Vivian asks, very worried.

"Lilith is dead, she died in the hospital from a house fire, doctors and nurses couldn't save her," Lansky says with a tear falling from her face.

Vivian wipes the tear from Lansky's face before speaking. "I'm sorry to hear this but your sister wouldn't want you to solve this case with sadness or remorse but with a hero's heart," Vivian says as she heads to her room.

Lansky walks out of the insane asylum and thinks about what her Aunt Vivian said as she gets in the car. She looks at the passenger seat and sees a blood rose with an eye on it. "Ew, what the-?" Lansky says as she picks up the blood rose and puts it in a ziplock bag along with the eye. "That's strange, what could this mean? All these clues point to one thing, but what?" Lansky asks herself as she starts the car and drives to the police station that's still being repaired. As she drives the car she stumbles across a dead body on the side of the road. "That's even more unnerving than earlier," Lansky says. She then parks in the parking lot of the police station, gets out of her car and walks inside.

A few hours went by and Judy stood in the forest searching for the house Lansky had told her about but it was nowhere to be found. As she walked, she felt something push her and could hear the laughter of children around her. "Who's there? Why are you doing this?" Judy said in a scared tone.

There was no response, no answer, not a sound, except the voices of children's laughter getting louder and louder.

"You know what I can take this, because Judy Lockes is not scared of nothing so whoever is out there, bring it on playa," Judy says, putting her hands up and making fists.

The children's laughter got quieter and quieter, there was nothing but silence. "That's what I thought, no one and I mean no one messes with me, " Judy says, putting her hands down and walking through the forest.

A cold breeze blew and fog approached, suddenly a house appeared, but not like any ordinary house. A small house with dust surrounding it, along with some vines and a crow sitting on top of a barrel on the porch.

Judy walks towards the house and as she does a child's voice is heard from inside the house. "Judy, you should have stayed away along with your friends and now you're too late, you should have left when you had the chance," the voice inside the house said, as the door opened by itself, and a dark force pulled Judy inside.

Back in the police station, Lansky had another problem to deal with, the new FBI agent who took over after her friend Effiney was killed. "Look Lansky, I don't care how this case went down, unless you have physical evidence stating that some supernatural being is the cause of this, I have no choice but to close this case and leave it as such," the agent says.

"I know it may sound crazy but if I could have just a moment of your time, I could show you the evidence my team and I have gathered," Lansky said.

"Fine but you have ten minutes and if it sounds like more nonsense, then you have to resign from commissioner and go back to being a detective following orders given by someone who can take this job seriously, now show me the evidence." The agent follows Lansky to her office.

"Okay so from what I've gathered I noticed a pattern. With each murder, that's been happening recently and even before that there was a flower said to have been a myth but no one has any proof it did, or didn't exist, until now," Lansky says, showing the FBI agent a blood rose inside an evidence bag.

"A rose? What does this have to do with the murders or this case?" the agent asked, looking at the rose in the bag.

"Right, sorry I got a little side tracked. Anyways the pattern I noticed is with each murder and this dates back to the seventeen hundreds to about now, that there is a blood rose left along with the victim's eyes but not the body," Lansky says pointing at pictures on the bulletin board.

"Whose victims?" the agent asked, very confused.

"Who I believe to be Lady Midnight also know as Karo Enika Medianoche, now I've looked at the pieces to this puzzle and I found each murder to be similar to the one before except this time this one was different, and this time it was Effiney Linadale who was killed," Lansky said.

"I don't get any of what you're saying. What does this have to do with anything?" the agent asks.

"Well the people that were murdered were in the Valentine family and I think I'm closer to cracking this case. When I put all the evidence I had together, I figured out that Lady Midnight is not targeting just any family but one, one that has been traced down to Alastair Valentine and Bethany Grace. The Valentines, but I'm so close to solving this case if you'll just give me more time, I'll go along with some officers if you-," Lansky said, being interrupted by the FBI agent.

"I think I heard enough, turn in your badge and forget about this case, don't think about solving it again. This is madness and one that can have you sent to the insane asylum just like your Aunt Vivian," the agent said leaving Lansky's office.

Lansky runs out and catches up to the FBI agent outside. "First of all my aunt wasn't crazy,and she doesn't belong there. Secondly, firing me is a huge mistake, and thirdly technically you can't take my badge away because you're an FBI agent not my boss." Lansky says.

"You may be right about two things but my statement still stands, and I can if the new mayor says so," the agent says, revealing her mayor's badge along with her FBI one.

"I did not see this coming," Lansky said, looking at the badge.

"So correct me again former Commissioner Lansky and you'll find yourself in the looney bin along with your aunt, you got that, dude?" the agent said, walking away to her car. Cassie pulls up in her black car and lowers the window. "Get in, Lansky," Cassie says as she unlocks the car door and opens it. Lansky walks over to Cassie's car, gets inside and then closes the car door.

As Lansky gets in the car she notices something sticking out of Cassie's bag in the backseat of her car. She pulls out a book from Cassie's bag in the back and puts it on her lap. "Where did you find this?" Lansky asked while Cassie started driving the car. "Oh, that, it's a book on the dark elves born on Christmas day but it doesn't make any sense because not all the elves in that book were born on Christmas day but anyways this is going to sound crazy but it fell off one of the shelves on its own and that's pretty much how I found it," Cassie said continuing to drive.

"Interesting, and not considering what we are up against, this doesn't sound crazy at all, but anywho any word from Judy?" Lansky asked.

"Um, no, I thought you would have heard from her because you two are colleagues at the police station," Cassie said.

"No, I haven't. That's why I asked you and about me being one of her colleagues at work, I had to resign because apparently everything I said was just nonsense. And I was told I sound like my crazy Aunt Vivian and she's not even crazy," Lansky says, opening the book and looking through it.

"I'm sorry that happened and if we don't hear back from Judy soon then we're doomed. We have no way of stopping Gladimere or Lady Midnight and there's no way we could stop Joelle either, so I'm just going to say it, we're screwed." Cassie says as she parks her car in her driveway at her house.

"Actually that's not entirely true, if you notice Gladimere can't touch a blood rose and we can use that to our advantage." Lansky says, taking a plastic bag out from her pocket with a blood rose and an eye in it. "Okay good point, but how are we going to stop the other two? We don't even know Lady Midnight's weakness, or how we're going to find the one thing that was taken from Joelle," Cassie says, getting out of the car.

"Well I did skim through some info on Joelle and you're not going to believe what I found," Lansky said following Cassie inside the house, carrying her stuff inside.

"What did you find?" Cassie asked, sitting on the couch, in her living room. "I read something that said Joelle had something taken from her, something valuable, something-," Lansky says, sitting down and opening the book. "Something like her antlers, it says here when something valuable is gone all things remain dark until it is returned," Lansky said.

"That sounds like a riddle, but it also doesn't make sense," Cassie said.

"It does, if you think about it, something was taken from her and when it was she went savage, rogue. So we need to find her antlers that were taken from her in order to stop her, but first we need to find Judy," Lansky said.

"Okay, while we're on this subject I snapped a picture of something and well look," Cassie said showing Lansky the picture she took on her phone.

"That woman holding the rose looks like Lady Midnight's mother, Evangeline Astraya. She wore the crown that Lady Midnight took from the museum. Now that I think about it, she didn't steal it if it already was supposed to be hers, it all makes sense now," Lansky says as memories from the past and present start flooding in.

"Lansky?.....Lansky?....Lansky!" Cassie shakes Lansky due to her not saying anything or moving. "What?, sorry I don't know what just happened but I know the answers, I know why she's doing all this. It all makes sense," Lansky said.

"What does? You do?" Cassie asked, very confused.

"Okay so, the security guard at the museum, the commissioner and the mayor, what do they all have in common?. All three of them were leaders or at least two of them were, but they were also related to the Valentines and the people that killed Karo Medianoche. Which, if you think about it, makes sense on why she's killing the bloodline of Valentines and not just them but the other four families that were also involved," Lansky explained. "So what you're saying is, Lady Midnight is killing them because of what those six people did to her and what does this have to do with the knights?" Cassie asked, confused as to what Lansky said about the knights.

"Well when Karo was a kid her mother was taken from her because of what Gladimere said and she never saw her mother again after that," Lansky said.

"How do you know this? None of what you are saying has been shown in the museum." Cassie asked.

"Trust me, I just know." Lansky said.

"Alright, now that we have some of the info we need, how are we going to find Judy?" Cassie asked.

"Well the last place she was at was in the forest looking for Gladimere's house, so we'll search there and after that we'll regroup and find Lady Midnight, Gladimere and Joelle, and stop them once and for all," Lansky said, closing the book.

"Okay I like your enthusiasm with this. I know this probably isn't the right time for me to ask but where did you get that necklace you're wearing around your neck?" Cassie asked.

"My aunt Vivian gave it to me, why?" Lansky asked, looking at her necklace and then at Cassie.

"No reason it just looks like the one Karo Enika Medianoche wore before she died and became what we refer to her as Lady Midnight now," Cassie said.

"Oh, okay, that's the same thing I told my aunt Vivian before I left the insane asylum," Lansky said.

"Oh, okay then, let's go find Judy before it's too late," Cassie said, heading to the door. Lansky and Cassie both walk out of the house and get in the car. Cassie starts driving and for a brief moment thinks about the information Lansky had told her about Joelle and Lady Midnight. "So how exactly are we going to find Judy and Joelles' antlers?" Cassie asked.

"Well if Judy is in the forest we'll have to stay together and not split up because you never know who or what we may find, and as for Joelle's antlers I think I may have seen them in the museum in one of the exhibits next to the hall of royals. I didn't think that they were important until now," Lansky said, looking at the bag with a rose and eye in it.

"Is that the blood rose you showed me earlier?" Cassie asked.

"Yeah, I forgot to mention I found these in my car before I got fired, it's strange because I don't know who put this there in the first place," Lansky said.

"Well if it was put in your car, it must have been given to you for a reason." Cassie said.

"But what reason would that be? Unless it was a message sent, but what could it mean?" Lansky asked. "I'm not sure but maybe it's a warning or something," Cassie said. "It's best to focus on finding Judy, getting the antlers for Joelle and then deal with the rest of our problems," she said, parking her car by the forest.

"Yeah you're probably right." Lansky said.

"We're here," Cassie said, pointing outside to the forest. Lansky nods and gets out of the car. Cassie gets out of the car as well and follows Joelle into the forest to look for Judy.

CHAPTER 10
The Broken Bond

Lansky and Cassie walk in the forest, searching for Judy. But she was nowhere to be found, the only thing found was the wind blowing and nothing but silence. Lansky pulls out her flashlight and turns it on. A branch breaking can be heard from the dark part of the forest. "Did you hear that?" Cassie asked.

"Yeah, it sounded like it was coming from the dark part of the forest, maybe that's where Judy is at," Lansky said, heading to the dark part of the forest.

"Yeah, maybe," Cassie said in a scared tone, following Lansky into the dark part of the forest. Lansky looks around the forest and looks for Judy.

As Cassie and Lansky walk through the forest, they approach a house and see a flashlight on the porch. "Look, there's a flashlight on the porch," Cassie says pointing at the flashlight on the porch.

Lansky walks up to the porch and looks at the flashlight. "That must mean Judy was or is here," Lansky said.

"Are you sure?" Cassie said walking on the porch.

"Yup, this flashlight has Judy's name on it and there's also footprints, so stay behind me at all times and make sure to stay close, we don't know what else we are dealing with in this house," Lansky said.

"Okay now let's go inside and get our friend Judy back," Cassie said.

Lansky nods as both her and Cassie walk inside the house. As they walk in the house, they start to look around. "This place is a little bit creepy," Cassie said.

"I know, I've been here but that's strange. There's usually a cauldron sitting in front of the door when you enter. No matter, look around and see if you can find anything that may lead to us, try finding Judy over in that room in the corner and I'll look over there to the right," Lansky said, walking in the room to the right of the house.

"Um, okay, I guess," Cassie says, walking into the room in the corner. Cassie looks around the room and searches for Judy, but nothing was there, just a dark blood rose sitting on top of the dresser. "Hmm, that's strange, well looks like Judy is not in here," Cassie says to herself while looking at the rose. She continues to look around and opens the closet, and to her surprise she finds a diary. She then takes the diary and looks through it. "Whoa, this looks like an old diary. I wonder who it belongs to," Cassie says as she looks at one of the pages. "I better show Lansky this," Cassie says walking out of the room with the diary and looks for Lansky.

Meanwhile, Lansky looked around the room separate from the one Cassie was in and looked for Judy. As she walked around she noticed a letter written by the same Lilith V. person that her and Effiney had found weeks ago. "Dear Karo, I tried finding you at the market place we were supposed to meet at but for some reason you didn't show up. I understand completely if you are having a bad day because I would too if I were being bullied for so long but anyways I ran into someone. Someone I didn't recognize, she seemed like a creature I hadn't seen before. She asked me about you. Of course I didn't tell her much except that your coronation is tomorrow and I may have accidentally invited her to it, please don't be mad at me. Sincerely, your friend Lilith V., " Lansky read the letter to herself. "That's the second time I've seen this name but who is this person and why do they have my sister's name?" Lanskey grabbed the letter and walked out to meet with Cassie to see if she found anything.

As Lansky walks out of the room she sees Cassie with a diary. "That's the same diary me and Effiney found before she died, but we never really thought to look at it," Lansky said. "Oh, I didn't know that, but I looked at one of the pages and it looked like someone must have written it a long time ago. I just don't know who it belongs to though," Cassie said. "Hmm, interesting. My guess is it belongs to Karo Enika Medianoche. Based on the initials on the front cover but that could explain how Gladimere knew so much about her," Lansky says, looking at the diary in Cassie's hand.

"How do you know?" Cassie asks.

"Well before my friend Effiney had died we did some investigating which led us here and she too found that diary you hold in your hands. But anyways, um after that me and Judy investigated the elderly home to see if anyone there knew anything and it turned out someone did but before they could tell us more about Gladimere they were killed and the strange thing is Judy had said the body was missing which makes me think that something suspicious is going on here. And everytime I investigate this case it's a constant reminder of the fact I was too late to save Effiney, even when I tried to not think about it, it still hurts. I know people have told me that it's not my fault but I can't help but think that everything that has happened so far is. My parents death from a house fire, my sister Lilith almost being put in the system because I was almost late coming into court, then her dying in the hospital from the same thing that happened to our parents. And finally someone who I never told them I was sorry for doubting them, Effiney, dying because I couldn't save them from some supernatural being who's probably going to kill Judy and then you, and everyone I care about. This is probably why I have a hard time getting close to people, because everytime I think I can trust someone the next thing you know, they're gone and I have myself to blame," Lansky said, feeling very emotional. "Oh, okay I had no idea any of this had happened. I mean I heard an officer had died but I didn't know it was your friend. And look those things may have happened but look how far you came from this, you believed in yourself and pretty much anyone you met or have known when no one would believe in them or you. I never thought we'd come this far either but we did and darn it our friend is depending on us to find her. What I'm trying to say is, that you shouldn't blame yourself for the bad things because in the end our lives will be miserable. It's not a good ending for this journey that still lies ahead," Cassie says, putting her hand on Lansky's shoulder and hugging her.

Lansky hugs her back. "You're right and this is probably not a good time for this because we have a friend to find and begin to stop," Lansky said.

"Good point, I couldn't find Judy in that room I was in, you?" Cassie asked. "No, but I did find a rose, the same one from all these murders and the one in that bag with the eye attached to it I found. That's all, but no Judy." Lansky said. "Okay well we shouldn't give up just yet. This house may be small but it's not like anyone can just disappear or hide." Cassie said, looking at the back door.

Lansky stood by the wall with more memories flooding back but this time it was as if it was a vision of the past or someone trying to tell her something. "Lansky?" Cassie shakes Lansky.

"Sorry I did it again,but anyways yeah you're right. Based on the blood on the floor, she must have gone past the back door and further into the forest." Lansky said.

"Okay then we'll go there then." Cassie said walking out the backdoor. Lansky follows Cassie out the back door and walks further into the forest. "So Lansky, what exactly is happening to you?" Cassie asked as she walked with Lansky further in the forest. "Visions, I've been seeing memories as well but someone else's, as if someone were trying to show me the truth about Karo…er…Lady Midnight and everything else that's happened. I don't know why, but it started to happen when you showed me that photo you took on your phone," Lansky said as she continued to walk.

"That's odd, I've heard of a seer but I never thought one existed. Maybe this isn't what this is but it could be," Cassie said.

"Maybe, but that probably isn't what it is, anyways did you notice those sticks over there, they kind of look like antlers which isn't at all…um..suspicious considering we're in a creepy forest," Lansky said.

"Yeah, you don't think those are the antlers that were… you know the thing taken from Joelle?" Cassie asked.

Lansky walked over to the sticks shaped like antlers with vines covering them. "I thought they'd be in the museum, I guess not…but why would they be here though?" Lansky asked.

"Beats me, I haven't the foggiest idea. But now that we have the antlers, now we just need a blood rose." Cassie said.

"I got that covered but stopping Lady Midnight is another problem we have to find a solution to," Lansky said, taking the vines off the antlers and carrying them.

"Okay, well let's not stop here just yet, let's keep walking further to see where this blood trail leads us," Cassie said.

Lansky nods. She then follows the blood trail with Cassie which leads them to another dark path. "This can't be good, maybe we should turn back," Cassie said.

"No, if we turn back then it will be too late to save everyone, including Judy," Lansky said. "So let's just keep walking until we figure out where this path leads." she says, as she continues to follow the path with Cassie while holding the antlers.

"Okay then," Cassie said.

She hears a woman humming from deep inside the forest. "Um Lansky?" Cassie said.

"No, we're not turning back," Lansky said.

"No it's not that um….did you hear someone humming?" Cassie asked.

"No,why?" Lansky asked.

"Because I thought I heard someone humming somewhere in the forest," Cassie said as she felt the cold breeze on her shoulder.

"Well that's strange, I didn't hear anything." Lansky said.

"Okay maybe I'm just hearing things," Cassie said.

A child's laughter was heard by Cassie and Lansky but for some reason the strange voices were only heard by Cassie.

"You're next," a voice said.

"You should have listened to the warnings before," another voice said.

"Is it time for us to run now?" Cassie asked.

"No- I'm not scared of any-," Lansky said, as a dead body dropped from one of the trees. "Okay now we can run," Lansky ran through the forest with Cassie while still following the dark path but as soon as she stopped to catch her breath, the voices and laughter stopped, and she and Cassie ended up in what seemed to have been a broken castle. "Whoa this is strange, I've only read about this in books, but I never thought it would be a broken castle years later," Cassie said.

"Well neither did I, and I also never thought this path would lead us here," Lansky said, walking around. Lansky walks inside the castle ruins and looks around. "No sign of Judy but that's strange the blood trail ends here," Lansky said.

"That doesn't make any sense unless it's because of the curse," Cassie said walking in the broken castle. "What curse?" Lansky asked.

"Well legend has it that there was a curse placed on this kingdom, basically before Evangeline was killed, she placed a curse on this kingdom, that if anyone were to harm the princess, this castle would fall apart, physically and emotionally. But that's only a legend, it couldn't be true," Cassie said.

"Well if Lady Midnight is really a supernatural being, then I'm afraid it may be, but that curse could explain why this castle is broken and fallen apart from the inside and out," Lansky said.

"Yeah, that's true. That could also explain why the blood trail has ended here. This castle is known to be very scary in some ways which is why no one has come here," Cassie said.

"Interesting, how bad was this curse?" Lansky asks.

"It was said to be so bad that my ancestors Alastair and Bethany had to move out of this castle and to what we now call the Holloway Museum," Cassie explained. "And that's not the worst part, the worst part was that this very spot is where Karo got struck by the knights and also the curse made this castle collapse, killing the lives within. But luckily there were alot of survivors," she continued.

"Well any chance you know how to break this curse or if there's a possibility Judy might be here?" Lansky asked.

"No one knows how to break this curse and there's a possibility she may be here," Cassie said.

A dark figure that's wearing a black cloak with a silver and navy blue belt,holding a staff with a crow on it along with a crown with a sparrow on top of its head, appears where Cassie and Lansky are standing. "Who dares enter this fortress, thou art definitely doomed, now for she will execute those who shall disturb her from getting revenge on the thieves that stole her reign from her," the figure said.

"We're not afraid of who you speak of, we know why she's doing this and we're here to stop her," Lansky said as her necklace started to glow.

"Thou wears the necklace of the moon goddess? That means either thou was chosen or thou stole it from ... Lady Midnight?" the figure said as it looked at the necklace glowing.

"I didn't steal it, it was given to me by one of my relatives," Lansky said. "I have been mistaken then, thou and thou friends shall continue to look for what has been lost but be warned I will not be so generous the next time we meet," the dark figure disappears.

"Well that was very creepy and unsettling," Cassie said.

"Yeah but also strange, we could have been killed by that figure but instead it left without harming us," Lansky said.

"Yeah and your necklace was also glowing which means you are ...nevermind," Cassie said.

"Oh, okay. I didn't realize it was glowing. Anyways we should probably look for clues to see where Judy is,"

Lansky said, as she heard a scream coming from upstairs in the broken castle she and Cassie were in. "Let's go, I heard a scream coming from upstairs of the castle," Lansky says, running up the stairs with Cassie. As they reach the top of the staircase the scream gets louder and louder. "This way Cassie," Lansky says, pointing to the room down the hallway. Cassie nods and follows Lansky to the room down the hall. They approach the room and the door opens by itself. They then walk in the room and see a closet open by itself. Someone walked slowly out of the closet, Lanskey pulled Cassie behind her as she pulled out her gun.

And there stood Lady Midnight holding a blood rose in her hand. She looks at Lansky and looks behind her, seeing Cassie. "You are next, Cassandra Valentine," Lady Midnight said, her voice echoing as it gets deeper and deeper. Lady Midnight rushes towards Cassie but as she does, she is blasted back by the light force coming from Lansky's necklace. "You stole my necklace from me, thief, traitor, ahhhhhh," Lady Midnight says as she screams so loud the walls start to crack.

She disappears through the walls and blood rose petals are left, creating a trail for Lansky and Cassie to follow. "She left a trail, maybe if we follow it we may find where she went," Lansky said.

"This must be where she was murdered," Cassie said.

"Come on, we don't have time for a detour, we have to save Judy and everyone else, we don't have time-," Lansky said, pulling on Cassie's arm and stopping, noticing the names on the wall. "These names must be the people that killed her." Lansky said. "It's not just my family it's also the other ones that murdered her too, were not just up against a powerful being but a queen who never got a happy ending, my ancestor, Bethany, and her friends ruined that for her, you're right we have to go, whatever happens I just want to say thank you for being my friend," Cassie said.

"Look your ancestor may have done bad things but that doesn't mean you deserve the same fate as her, no one does, now we have some beings to stop," Lansky said, placing the antlers in her bag. Lansky and Cassie follow the blood rose trail which leads them to the throne room of the castle. Lansky picks up a sword from the throne room floor. "Here you're going to need this," Lansky said, handing the sword to Cassie. Cassie then takes the sword and carries it as she and Lansky walk around the throne room.

Joelle appears sitting on the throne smirking as she sees Lansky and Cassie. "So now it's down to two, well unfortunately your friend Judy is right here" Joelle said, using her magic to make Judy appear tied up and with cuts on her. Judy runs over to Lansky and Cassie.

"Judy, I'm so glad you're alive," Lansky said.

"Same, but now is not a good time for a reunion," Judy says.

Gladimere appears standing next to the throne Joelle is sitting at. "You're too late," Gladimere said.

"You just couldn't stay away could you, Lansky," Joelle said.

Lady Midnight appears with her black hair up in a ponytail, her black veil out of her face, wearing an emerald crown with a chain wrapped around her ponytail, wearing a black dress and her red jacket. She stands in the middle of the throne room. "You should have listened to the warning and now you're too late," Lady Midnight says as she makes the swords from the armor of the knight statues float towards Cassie and Lansky. The swords scratch Cassie and Judy, making them fall to the ground.

Lansky puts her bag down and walks over to Cassie and Judy. "You two get out of here, I'll stop them," Lansky said.

"No, we started this together and I want to finish it together," Judy says, as she gets up with Cassie. "Very well then," Lansky said. As Lansky picks up her bag, antlers fall out of it. Joelle appears in front of Lansky. "Take them, they belong to you," Lansky said.

"No, I will not take anything from you, now Gladimere starts the spell," Joelle says.

Gladimere uses her magic to create a magic storm surrounding Lansky, Cassie and Judy.

"Please Joelle, you can stop this, you are so much more than this," Lansky said. "My father never appreciated me so why should ANYONE ELSE," Joelle said yelling the last part and throwing a magic blast at Lansky. Lansky falls to the ground and tries to get back up again.

Lady Midnight attacks Cassie. Cassie tries fighting back with the sword in her hands.

Gladimere pushes Judy with her staff while Judy fires her gun at her. Lansky looks at Judy and then at Cassie.

She hears a voice tell her "your friends need you, the battle is not done yet." She then gets up and her eyes glow a blue color as she feels the soul of another being float inside her.

"I will not let any of you take my friends," said Lansky.

"Ha, you think you and your friends can stop us, you're sadly mistaken."Joelle said. "From pure hearts to one, I will not let the darkness destroy the light from the battle that's begun," Lansky said, tripping Joelle. Joelle falls to the ground and Lansky runs over to Judy. Lansky pulls out a blood rose from her pocket and looks at Gladimere.

"That rose cannot stop me." Gladimere said.

"It's not just any rose, it is a blood rose. Something you fear, but I didn't know why until now," Lansky said as her clothes changed into a queen's clothing.

"No, no, you can't be," Gladimere said. "You can't make me…touch the blood rose," Gladimere cried out.

Lansky tosses the blood rose at Gladimere. Gladimere catches the rose with her hand. "Ha, nothing happened," Gladimere said. A door from the corner of the throne room opens. Footsteps were heard and a figure walked into the throne room. The magic storm stopped and disappeared. "What have you done!" Gladimere yells at Lansky. The figure appears wearing a cape with a hood over its head. Lady Midnight stops fighting Cassie and walks over to the figure. Joelle gets up and picks up a sword off the ground. "No, if I don't get to live then no one does." Joelle yells, as she runs at Cassie and stabs her with a sword in her hand.

Lansky looks over at Cassie. "NOOOOO!" Lansky yelled.

Gladimere and Judy look over at the figure. The figure takes their hood off their head and takes the cape off, revealing Evangeline Astraya…Lady Midnight's mother. Lady

Midnight looks at her mother and a tear falls from her face.

"You're not supposed to be here, I didn't mean to take the antlers from that girl and I never meant for your daughter to be this being, please no…dont send me back," Gladimere said, as Evangeline drags her to a prison realm for the wicked and evil beings of the world.

Lansky catches Cassie as she falls. "I'm not going to let you die on me," Lansky says. "We both knew this fate would come, I'm destined to die," Cassie said, bleeding out from where she was stabbed.

Joelle notices the antlers glowing on the floor and she puts the sword down. She picks up the antlers and the antlers reappear on her head. "Lansky I am sorry for all of this, it was Gladimere all along who was a horrible person, she wanted me to do all this just so she could use Karo and ruin her life," Joelle said.

"It's fine, something was stolen from you and you are not to be blamed," Lansky said as the soul inside her came out and appeared as a ghost of a girl with short black hair, wearing a magenta dress and a bow in her hair.

"You did it, Lansky, you stopped the evil and now it is my time to move on from this world and go to the after life," the ghost girl said.

"What about Lady Midnight?" Lansky asked.

Lady Midnight looks at the ghost girl and then disappears in the shadows.

"She may be free from Gladimere but not yet ready to move on to the afterlife, it appears something else may be missing from her but not something you should worry about now," the ghost girl says, fading away.

Lansky then looked at Cassie, her wound was healed. "Is it all over?" Cassie asked.

"For now it is over, let's go," Lansky said. Cassie gets up and walks out of the castle with Judy and Lansky.

Joelle catches up with them. "Wait, Lansky," Joelle said.

"Yeah, Joelle?" Lansky asked.

"Thank you for freeing me and Karo. I must go now," Joelle said, as her body disappeared in snowflakes. "Goodbye Joelle," Lansky said.

"So where to now?" Cassie asked.

"I'm not sure but Holloway needs me because there may be other dark forces that lie ahead and who knows if Gladimere or Lady Midnight will come back," Lansky said, as her clothes went back to her detective clothes.

"Your right playa," Judy said.

A few years had passed and Lansky had got her job back, Judy became deputy, Cassie became the owner of the Holloway Museum and Lansky's Aunt Vivian was free from being at the insane asylum. At the museum, Lansky stood near an exhibit with relics in the hall of ancient relics exhibit, and there lies the book of Wisterian along with the staff of Malaysia.

A woman wearing a hood approached Lansky. "Kea Lansky, can we talk?" the woman asked.

"Yeah, um how do you know my name?" Lansky asked.

"It's a long story, but I believe we have met before. Anyways, there's something I need to tell you," the woman said.

"What's that?" Lansky asked.

"You're a descendant of Lady Midnight and that's why that magic helped you when you needed it the most," the woman said.

"That's impossible, Karo never had any children," Lansky said.

"No, but her younger sister did," the woman said.

"Her younger sister is dead, long gone," Lansky said.

"Or is she?" the woman said, taking her hood off and revealing herself.

"Lacey Gunderson, but how?" Lansky said.

"I'll explain later but for now there's something we have to do, and my name is Keira Medianoche," Lacey said.

Lansky and Keira walk out of the museum. A few hours later the museum had closed and two of the relics in the hall of ancient relics glowed, the Staff of Malaysia and the Book of Wisterian. A man with a monocle appears by a relic that seems to be a cowboy hat as lightning flashed from the storm outside.

THE END

ABOUT THE AUTHOR

Hello, my name is Mariah Archibeque and I have been writing my own stories for as long as I can remember. This book is the only one I dreamed about getting published mainly because some of them are unfinished or scrapped. I was inspired to write this story partially based on my life. Growing up I was picked on and I had no idea how to deal with it. But that was until people told me that I am a strong, independent young woman.

I am nineteen years old and this story holds a special place in my heart. One of the quotes I came up with that reminds me of this story is "You can't change a butterfly into something ugly." In other words you shouldn't be something you are not. This story reminds me of one of the main characters in this book which would be none other than Kea Lansky. In conclusion, this story is something I am very proud of writing and one that I admire.

www.ingramcontent.com/pod-product-compliance
Lightning Source LLC
Chambersburg PA
CBHW041738300726
48978CB00006B/154